BLOOMFIELD TOWNSHIP PUBLIC LIBRARY
W9-BWS-071

HELEN V. GRIFFITH

Plunk's Dreams

PICTURES BY
SUSAN CONDIE LAMB

GREENWILLOW BOOKS, New York

Watercolor paints and pencil with gesso were used for the full-color art.
The text type is ITC Zapf International Medium.

Printed in Singapore by Tien Wah Press
First Edition 10 9 8 7 6 5 4 3 2 1

Library of Congress Cataloging-in-Publication Data

Griffith, Helen V.
Plunk's dreams / Helen V. Griffith; pictures by Susan Condie Lamb.
p. cm.
Summary: John imagines what vivid adventures may lie
in the dreams of his dog Plunk.
ISBN 0-688-08812-0. ISBN 0-688-08813-9 (lib. bdg.)
[1. Dogs—Fiction. 2. Dreams—Fiction. 3. Imagination—Fiction.]
I. Lamb, Susan Condie, ill. II. Title.
PZ7.G8823P1 1990 [E]—dc19 88-34905 CIP AC

FOR BUDDY

—H.V.G.

FOR CHRIS AND BARNEY

—S.C.L.

My dog dreams.
I know he does because sometimes when
he's lying on his side with his eyes tight shut,
he shakes his paws and wiggles his nose
and goes "Woof" in a tiny voice.

Then I say, “Plunk is dreaming.”
And Dad says, “He thinks he’s chasing rabbits.”
And Mom says, “He thinks he’s getting dinner.”
But that’s not what I think.

I think Plunk is dreaming that he's an Indian dog,

and he lives in the woods and travels in a canoe,

and he stays outdoors all the time and explores,
and he finds his own food and has a fire at night,

and sometimes he sees wild animals, but he's not afraid.

And when he wakes up

he'll think about how much fun he had, and
he'll want to go camping somewhere for real,
and I'd go, too, if somebody would take us.
That's what I think.

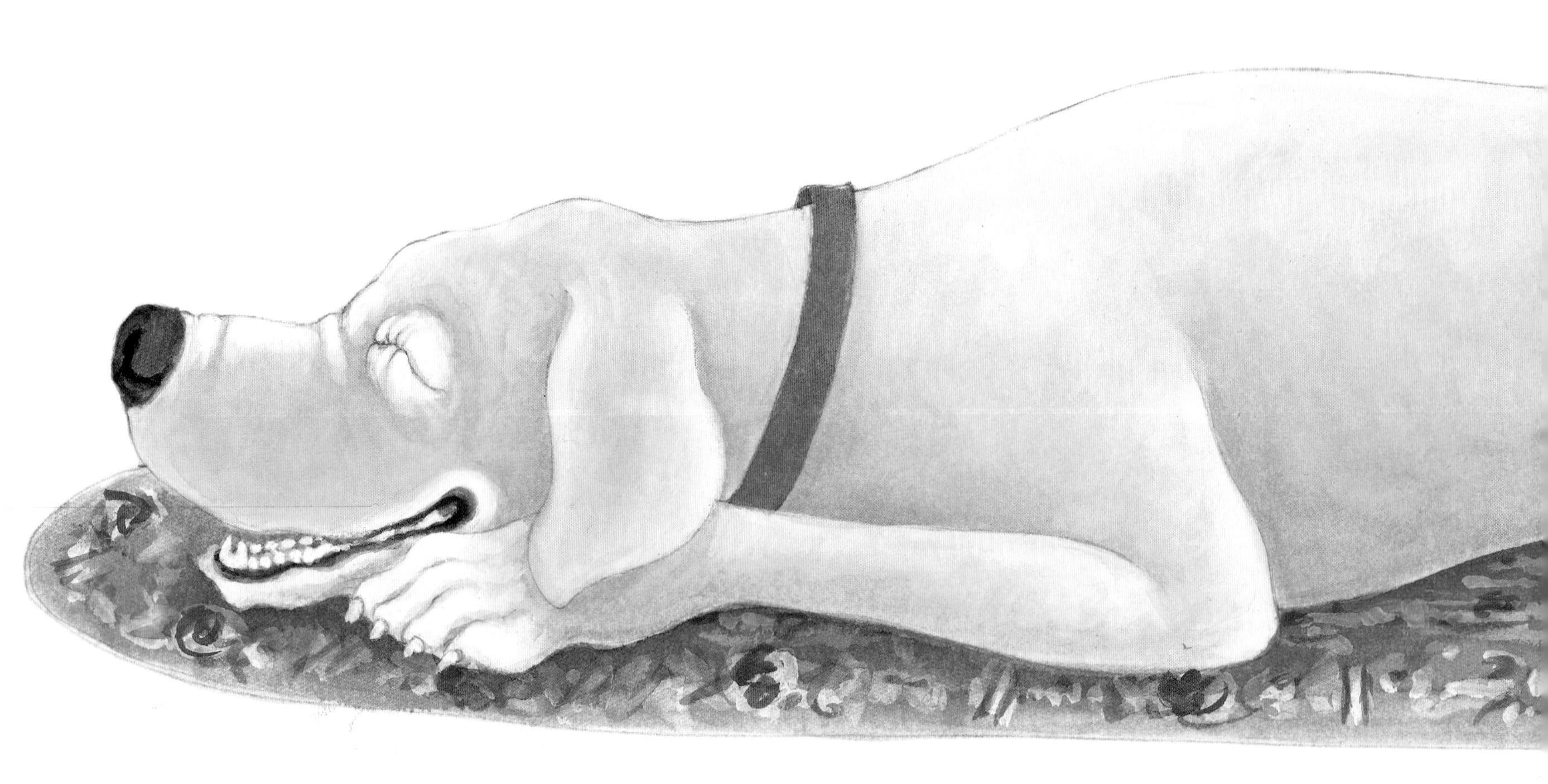

Sometimes when Plunk is asleep he makes
little yelps like this: "Yelp, yelp, yelp."
Then Dad says to me, "Look, John, Plunk
is chasing rabbits."

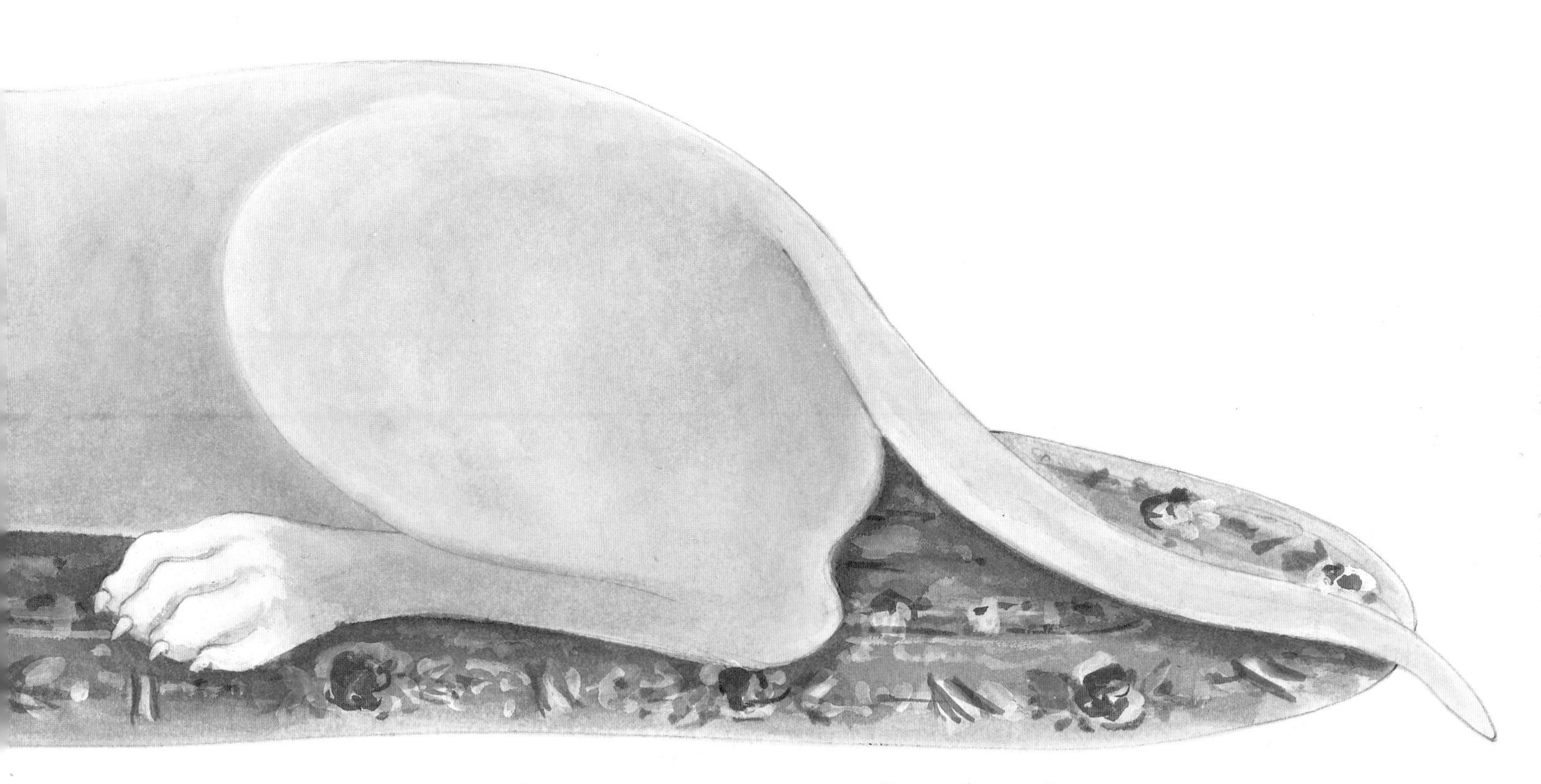

And Mom says to me, "Look, John,
Plunk is dreaming of dinner."
But that's not what I think.

I think he's dreaming that a spaceship has landed in
our yard, and he's barking to warn us of danger

and to scare away the aliens
who are climbing out of the ship,

but the aliens turn out to be dogs just like Plunk,
and they all talk together in dog language,

and they invite Plunk to come and live on their planet, but Plunk says he'd rather live here.

And when he wakes up

I'll give him some ice cream, and I'll probably have some, too.
That's what I think.

Sometimes when Plunk is sleeping he moves all four of his legs, and he looks like he's running, only he's lying down.

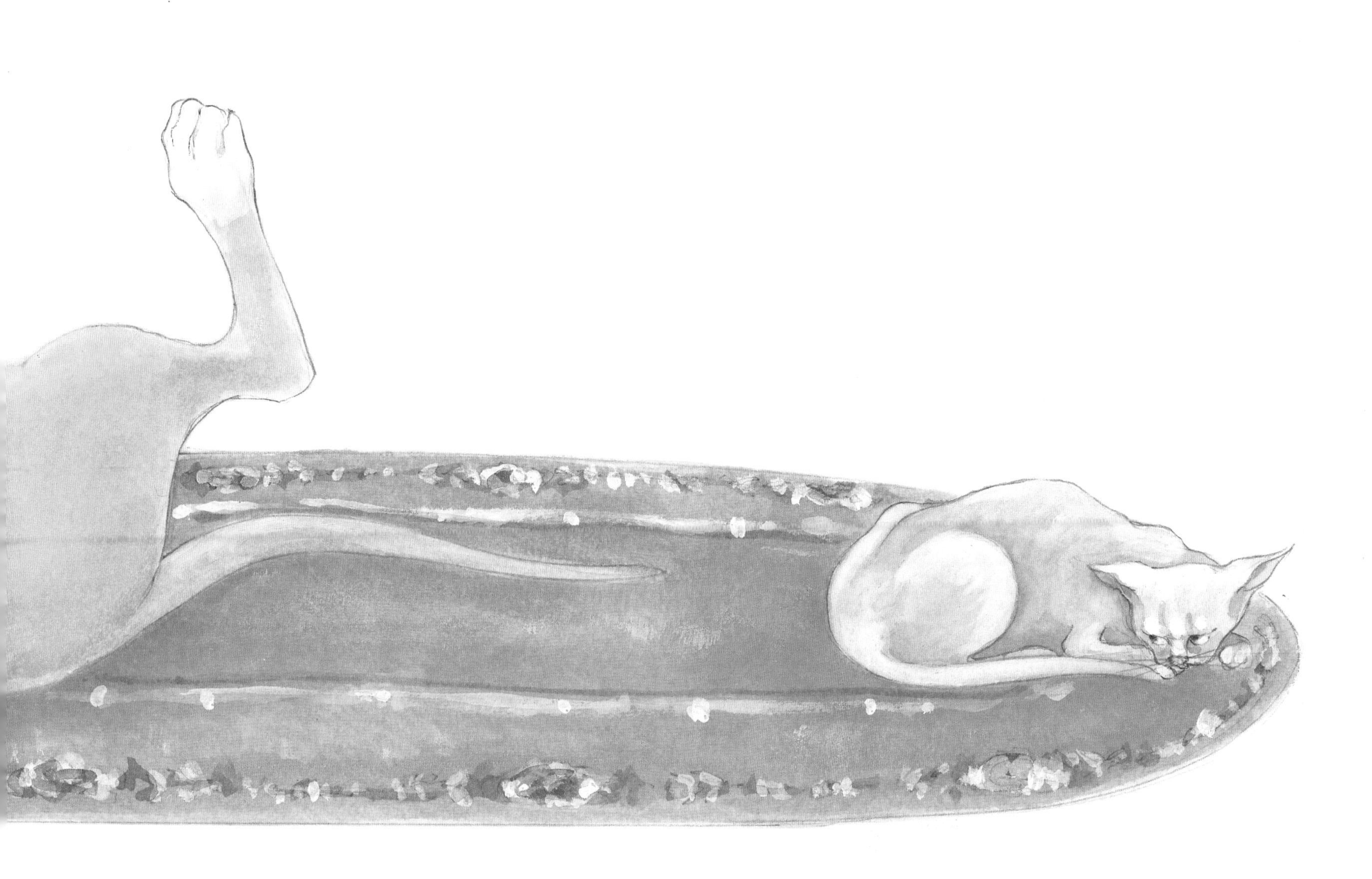

Then Dad says, “Chasing rabbits again.”
And Mom says, “Running for his dinner.”
But that’s not what I think.

I think he's dreaming that he's chasing our cat,
because he's not allowed to do that when he's awake,

and he's chasing her through the house and through the yard
and down the street, and while they're running

the cat gets bigger and bigger

until she's bigger than Plunk,

and all at once she turns around and starts to chase him,

and he tries to run, but his paws keep sticking to the ground,
and just as the cat reaches out her claws to grab him,

he'll wake up.

And when he does he'll be scared, because he won't
be sure whether he was dreaming or not, and he'll have
to sleep in my bed with me until he's not scared anymore.
That's what I think.

And then sometimes when Plunk is sleeping his sides quiver, and his tail goes *flop, flop* against the floor, and his lips wrinkle up so that he looks like he's smiling.

Then Dad says, “Look, Plunk is dreaming about John.”
And Mom says, “Plunk is dreaming about you, John.”

And that's what I think, too.